Running Away

to HOME

a verse novel

LITA HOOPER

BOOK ONE OF THE JOURNEY TRILOGY

Running Away to Home

a verse novel

Copyright © 2016 by Lita Hooper

Cover design by Aquarius Press

Author photo: Lita Hooper

ISBN 978-0-9971996-7-3

LCCN 2016951742

BRAVE BOOKS, a division of Aquarius Press

www.BraveBooks.net

Printed in the United States of America

*For my children — Malik, Demarko, and Sojourner —
and all the children lost and found in Katrina's wake.*

Contents

Chapter 1

Swerve

—Ronnie

Everybody on my block is about to die.

The news lady is saying, *Go to the Dome.*

Too late. We have waited too long.

The levees have broken!

She doesn't even blink when she says it.

Every night I watch the news with Daddy.

I know this news lady well.

Her dark clothes, her white smile, her stiff hair.

Today, urgency swells her eyes.

She wants to get off the air

rush to the Dome, feel her hair swirl

about her round, pale face.

I look at my sister, Sammie.

She is painting her nails

as if she's on vacation

poolside at a resort.

Daddy slumps in his favorite chair—

his hand barely holds his fourth drink.

It's perched on the worn arm

of the Lazy Boy. Jack Daniels

has Daddy thinking the Dome can wait.

Am I dreaming?

The living room seems slanted now.

Maybe I am in Daddy's dream.

Wake up, Daddy!

I reach out to touch something —

try to steady this roller coaster.

The air is wet. Katrina has broken the levees

pouring water into the Ninth Ward.

She is too real to sleep away, this Katrina.

I hear soprano cries

from down the street.

Or is it the wind?

Then silence, the worst kind.

 Through the living room window

I stare at the neighbors.

They do not stop to notice me.

They grab children, load black garbage bags

into trucks and cars. They pile into anything that moves

as the water makes a lake of our street.

Little patches of grass in each yard surrender.

But Daddy, Sammie, and I hold fort.

Trickle

—Sammie

Water is so quiet, ain't it?

Even when it creep up on you.

You know it's just water

tickling your toes. I like the way it feel.

Just like the water in the park swimming pool

when I dip my feet in just a little.

Now our house is a pool.

That water is snaking up my leg like a itch

trying to mess up my nails.

Stuff floating around like it don't belong to nobody:

Squishy stuffed animals, books, pillows.

Daddy is up now. His eyes is red as usual.

The water is a cold, wet blanket.

I don't like being cold. Or wet.

I should go get my yearbook.

But Daddy's voice is like thunder.

Samantha, leave that thing! BOOM!

What you need it for? You in twelfth grade now. BOOM! BOOM!

He don't know this is the first time me and Ronnie

have our own yearbooks.

No sharing this year.

Mamma use to say twins share everything

even heartbeats. I want my own heart.

And my own yearbook.

We walk real slow through the water.

Splashing like backtalk.

Ronnie stops me from falling.

I feel small today. Little-girl small.

Daddy put some stuff in a garbage bag.

And he got his camera bag.

He look funny holding them over his head

yelling at us like we about to die

if we don't move faster.

Come on, girls! Veronique! Samantha! We got to get going!

I know he don't want to go nowhere, though.

I keep looking at Ronnie

but she won't look back.

Departure

—Wilson

That crazy girl. She's trying to take a yearbook when this place is filling
up like a fishbowl. We can drown waiting on her. Still, I know why she
wants it. I'm thinking about that family portrait that used to sit on top of
the tv. I saw it float to the back room. I fight the urge to get it. I know I
have to keep something about how we were before today. What's better
than a picture of all of us? Velma, with her long, black hair. That dark
chocolate skin. Those big, brown eyes. My beautiful Velma. The girls
look just like her. I used to tease them and call them my triplets. That
was before I grew a beard and lost twenty pounds. In that picture, I'm
standing right beside my wife, head held high. Slight mustache, honey
brown skin like my father. My mother used to say Ronnie and Sammie
were a cross between us. Tall like Velma's folks, always looked older
than their age. Identical twins. But I've never had a problem telling
them apart. Velma said that was 'cause parents *know their children like
they know their own hearts.* Maybe 'cause of their personalities. Today
Veronique is in charge, as usual. No time to spare. The whole Ninth
Ward is filling up with water. Samantha keeps complaining and crying.
As usual.

Cross Current

—Ronnie

It is so windy and wet. I wish it was quiet like

the library when it opens. Daddy keeps saying

they will come. But who is he talking about?

I can tell he's not quite sure. The Dome is too far.

so we have to go to the church.

Junk and mud and people surround us.

Mr. Raymond's dogs are stranded on top of a car.

I want to help them, watch as

they pace on the roof. They are

deciding if the jump will be worth it.

I want to scream, *Jump! Jump!*

They look like wild animals, not yard dogs.

Daddy says God will protect them.

That makes Sammie feel better

but I know better.

Just three blocks from our house

we can't walk anymore.

A man yells *Get in!*

His rowboat is piled with

suitcases, a tv and a pillow.

The tv is tossed for us.

Murky water ripples like the wave in my chest.

Sammie smiles. She is on a roller coaster.

I can see the fantasy in her shiny eyes.

This is a game to her.

Then her wet hand is on my ear.

I got Mamma's picture, she says.

She says it like a secret

then points to her plastic bag.

Pose

—Sammie

Daddy took this picture of Mamma

on a hot Sunday. I remember she was

standing in the front yard

dressed for church:

red and yellow dress, big floppy hat.

She was waiting for us to come out.

Daddy said, *Let me take your picture, Velma. Come on, baby.*

Then he smiled dimple deep.

Mamma wouldn't stand near the tree.

She kept waving her hands.

Sammie and Ronnie, tell your mamma to listen to me!

I put my finger in Daddy's dimple.

Mamma's hands was in the air

like those women at church

who shout every week 'cause Jesus

is standing over them.

They look like they 'bout to lose their minds.

Twins, don't listen to him.

She always called us that.

Like we had one name.

Daddy didn't look drunk that day.

No falling down or

silly smile this time. Just his serious face.

Telling Mamma where to stand.

How to pose.

Patience

—Ronnie

Reverend Taylor and some church members

are yelling out to us from the rooftop of the church.

They are waving their hands like cruise boat passengers

saying goodbye. But nobody is going anywhere today.

Some people have candy, chips, and canned food.

All I can think of is a can opener.

How many of them remembered a can opener?

What's the point of bringing canned goods

if you can't open them?

I ask Daddy about getting some food.

He slides down on the gravel like his spine has given out.

Sammie keeps poking around in her plastic bag.

She smacks her gum and checks her nails every two minutes.

Before we left the house, I stuffed an old Wal-Mart bag

with my favorite book, *The Color Purple,*

two shirts, a toothbrush, socks, and three pairs of panties.

And Mamma's favorite necklace.

I start thinking of our lot, how it must look now.

After Mamma's funeral

Daddy was always at Summer Hill,

our family's land. It's the only thing he owned.

He always reminds us of that.

I don't own our house, and I don't own no car.

But I got land. It's our family land and it ain't going nowhere!

It's been our family's lot since slavery ended.

One white landowner's guilt kept Daddy sane.

Every Thanksgiving Daddy describes the same dream:

Our whole family at Summer Hill

      a big house, a yard, a covered porch.

      cousins, uncles, everybody.

Then Sammie asks, *Who are you talking about? We got family somewhere?*

Daddy gets real quiet. He never answers her.

There never seems to be never enough money

to do anything with the land. He pays the taxes.

Mows the lawn. And the lot waits every year

for our family to return and claim it.

Guess we have learned to wait, too.

Thief

—Wilson

Braver than me. My girls. I just don't know what to do. That's why my Ronnie took over. Even packed up the bags. I grabbed my camera and a bottle of Jack Daniel. *So stupid.* Didn't seem like a big deal on the tv. I've seen plenty of storms. Just figured we could wait it out. I don't want my girls down at the Dome. No telling what is going on down there. But when the water came through the front door like a quiet thief, I knew. Hell! I had waited too long. *Too damned long.* Now it feels like we've been robbed. We had no choice in the matter. That water just came right in and took everything. Seems like I'm always losing things, no matter how careful I am. I keep thinking about Velma, how she would've made sure we got out in time. Yes, she would have had a plan. She would be here taking care of all of us.

Mistake

—Sammie

Ronnie getting on my nerves!

Shoot! Everybody getting on my nerves.

That lady with them

kids keep crying, her kids

running all around

like nothing wrong.

Just play play play.

Must be five hours now.

I'm sick of sitting on these hot rocks

Where is the police?

And that girl from school, Shaneika Simmons

act like she don't know me.

Why can't we go to the Dome?

That's where we

supposed to be.

Enough

—Wilson

I need a drink. One bottle, that's all I grabbed. Man, we are sitting on this rooftop like some refugees in a foreign land. My girls look at me for answers I can't give. *When they coming, Daddy? Will we die here, Daddy?* The other parents just cry, holding their babies. Like that will do any good. I close my eyes, think about the day I bought a little swimming pool for the girls. They had to be three, maybe four. Velma said we couldn't go to the park. *No public pool, Wilson.* So I bought an inflatable pool, enough room for us all. Velma laughed so hard, she fell to her knees. Neighbors stared like I had dug a hole in the yard and put a real pool in. Never liked them fools. Always settling. Settling for a small life, no dreams. I blew that thing up, then we splashed around for hours. Didn't need a big pool. Didn't need nothing but us.

Rescue

—Ronnie

Even Reverend Taylor has left to go to the Dome.

But first he prayed with us. I don't think anybody

in that prayer circle ever prayed harder.

The heat pushes us down, even the little kids.

Daddy has found a spot with some shade

but we have to share it with three other people.

An older lady tries to sit with us

but there is no room. I give her my seat.

I don't want to sit next to Daddy anymore.

The sweetness of his whisky breath

makes me sick. I move to the edge of the building

near a rusty metal pipe, turn away from everyone.

The sun is at my back.

The wind hiccups. Louder and louder.

Now I can hear the choppy sound of air from a distance.

The helicopter! Sammie shouts, *They coming! They coming!*

She is waving one of my shirts high above her head.

She is smiling and crying, wiping her eyes and jumping.

But Daddy will not move.

In his eyes I can see that missing-man look.

They circle twice. The noise and wind are closer.

The helicopter is like a giant ceiling fan.

The guard grabs my wrist with his oversized hand.

My stomach flips, and I am giddy like Sammie on her roller coaster.

Daddy is in my face, pulling me toward him.

Ronnie, don't lose each other! They said to meet at Summer Hill!

Who? I yelled. My hair is flying hard against my face.

The reunion! The ancestors! Don't forget! he shouts.

I feel a hand on my shoulder.

It's a white man with dark sunglasses.

Sammie is already in the helicopter, smiling.

The white man grabs my hand again.

Then I am in the small seat next to Sammie.

When I look for Daddy, his back is turned.

He looks like a little boy hiding in a closet.

I want to reach for him.

In my head I am screaming, *Come with us, Daddy!*

But my throat is clenched in an endless swallow.

We lift up high above the others on

the rooftops of the city. They are waving shirts

that turn to flecks of paper as we float away.

Chapter 2

Surprise

—Sammie

It's crazy to think about leaving home.

I ain't been too many places.

Florida one time

but we was so little

I don't even remember.

Just these little palm trees.

I remember asking why they was so short.

On tv they was always so tall.

Daddy said sometimes nature surprise you.

Now the big surprise is this Katrina.

Pushing us out of town

into a shelter. Ain't nothing but a high school gym.

Nicer than our school. They say we can't leave though.

For your own safety.

They gave us sandwiches and soda.

They gave us some clothes, too. I got lucky.

Found jeans and two cute tops.

Ronnie say find a long sleeve shirt. I'm not listening.

What we need with some hot clothes? We'll be home

in a day or two anyway. They want us to sign a lot of papers.

Ronnie does that stuff for me. She always want to prove

how smart she is. That's why she always makes honor roll

and the teachers like her.

Ronnie say we got to find Daddy.

Tomorrow. Let's look tomorrow, I say.

I just want to sleep.

Ronnie keep saying we can't stay here forever.

It's too noisy and crowded in this gym.

I see some kids from school with their families.

Everybody look busy doing nothing.

In the corner, a group of old ladies

pray and sing church songs.

Every day I think it's the last day.

Men from the bus help people

when they check in.

They just keep coming and coming.

All dirty and lost looking.

The men bring cots out of nowhere.

Them thin cots that make your back hurt.

I wonder if Daddy got a cot wherever he is.

When will it be the last day?

Wish

—Ronnie

A shelter is like a prison.

Everybody thinks they don't belong here.

But we do. The Red Cross helps

but they can't stop the wave of pain in my chest.

With every breath, it swells like a tidal wave.

There are kids at the shelter, most without

parents: wild and wide-eyed.

They stare at the door to make their parents come.

There are parents crying for missing kids.

Some flash anger with every move.

Sometimes the noise rises to a mumbling

mess of laughter, crying and yelling, then

there is a silence that teeters

on the edge of an outburst.

No one can tell us what we need to know.

A woman from Chicago

said she had seen us on tv.

She drove for hours

to get here. For a few minutes

that wave eases to a soft current.

I think about my room. My books.

My honors certificates and trophies.

There's so much to clean up.

Whenever we get home, that's what I'll do.

Clean up.

Dreams

— Sammie

At night I hear people sneaking

out the gym. Kids our age sit in the hallway

trading clothes. Some of the grown-ups hang outside

playing cards, talking about the president.

Everybody inside the gym just sit up

 crying or praying.

It smell like the old folks home

my grandmother use to live in.

I call it the nut house

'cause everybody look

crazy, but my grandmother loved it there.

She even took care of the really sick people--

the ones who never had no visitors.

Daddy wanted her to live with us

but we didn't have enough room.

That's why we have Summer Hill.

When I was little, I use to think we

owned a mansion called Summer Hill.

I daydreamed about being rich.

Having maids and stuff.

I use to daydream a lot.

Surrogate

—Ronnie

It's been a week in the shelter. The longest

week I'll ever know. Today we were told

we can go to another city. Just like that.

Like being released from prison without a plan.

Two of the ladies tell us to get on the bus to Atlanta.

They say too many people are on the Houston bus.

They remind me of my grandmother.

They smile up at me and Sammy

like we belong to them somehow.

Sammie is begging me to get on that bus.

What would Mamma say? I think.

The wave in my chest begins to swell.

I have to decide. I remember when Sammie was sick

on the same day as my history exam.

Daddy was passed out in the back.

Sammie was throwing up. Her cries grew louder

but Daddy never moved.

A fever made her clammy and wet.

Mamma! I want Mamma! she yelled.

But Mamma had passed.

So I took her to the clinic.

The nurse looked us over

then asked about our parents

the way adults ask questions to trap you in a lie.

Our father works out of state, Miss Adams, I said.

Sammie coughed right on time.

Miss Adams sent her home.

But my history teacher didn't care

about my sister or the flu.

Snap

—Wilson

One week already. I wake up every night thinking about the girls. Had to put them on that helicopter. Had to. When those troopers came back, I told them to take their time. They called it in: *Suicidal.* Don't know what I was thinking. Felt like my head was flooding, just like the whole damned city. Death came to us on that rooftop. I wasn't going to let it take my girls. Not like I let it take Velma.

The wind smacked me around so much, I had to think straight. Then I dropped that bottle of Jack, held on to my camera strap. My loyal camera. Now I'm here at some shelter for the sick and crazy. Serves me right. Everybody is either lying on their back or talking to air. Or God. I talk to the camera. Only one digital card left. That's 500 pictures. Don't matter. Everyday I've been taking pictures of everybody around me. Feels good to have something to do. Some folks smile. One girl looks like my Sammie. A little younger, like the way she used to look when she sat up all night talking with me. My special girl. My girls.

Folks from the Red Cross promise everyday. *We'll find them, Mr. Baudean. We'll find them.*

Journey

—Sammie

Ronnie is finally getting on the bus.

Didn't mean to make her cry.

She cry like it don't matter

wipe her tears so fast

you hardly know she sad.

Not me. I cry loud and long.

Mamma always heard me.

Ronnie don't know everything.

She don't know me like she think.

Just like she didn't know when Mamma

was going to die. Didn't know this Katrina

was coming. And she don't know what's in Atlanta.

But Mamma told me to go.

Came to me in a dream.

Her soft voice said, *Keep moving.*

I told Ronnie about it this morning.

She said Mamma didn't visit her dreams.

Future

—Ronnie

Before this, I was college-bound.

Chicago or New York.

I want to see how other people live, like how they

ride the subway, walk long streets bordered by skyscrapers.

In daydreams I am at a law firm

in a blue suit, running to court, grabbing a cab.

Then I wake up:

How could Daddy do without me?

What did he say before the helicopter came?

The wave in my chest roars like the heavy bus engine

 as we pull onto the expressway.

Hangin'

—Sammie

In Atlanta we wait in long lines

in some community center.

These houses and cars make me think of home.

Mamma use to say the places black people stay

look the same everywhere.

Everything look unfinished

or thrown away.

They give us water, not soda.

I found a machine, but Ronnie is holding our money.

One dollar. Just enough for a candy bar.

Does the money have names on it?

One minute between us when we was born.

That's the only difference.

Longest minute of my life.

Music is coming from the parking lot.

I can see kids hanging out. Being kids.

Ronnie look so tired. I don't want to ask.

Because I Said So

—Ronnie

She is always up to something. Sammie can't see the danger

in situations. Just the fun. We are stuck in this city

without Daddy, without money, without a plan.

She wants to hang out in the parking lot

with a bunch of kids. I am sweaty and tired.

The air in this place is heavy. She is yelling at me about

not letting her have fun. Her hair is sticking up around her forhead.

For a second, I want to laugh, but I know that she

will start to cry if I do.

You need to stop acting like a baby, Sammie! We need to concentrate!

Shut up, Ronnie! I hate you! You all the time trying to tell me what to do.

I'm Free

—Sammie

When Ronnie gets all bossy, she gets mean.

She kept bossing me around. She pulled my arm

and that's when I snapped. She think she all that.

I told her to stop telling me what to do.

She got all mad and said she was in charge.

But I didn't hear Daddy say that when we left him on that roof.

All he said was…well, I don't know what he told her.

But he know I can take care of myself.

Maybe

—Ronnie

Sammie is heading to the parking lot.

The closer she gets to the music

the harder her waist twists to the rhythm.

Then her snapping fingers are in the air.

Through the dirty window I watch her blend into the crowd.

I see kids leaning into parked cars, pants sagging to mid-thigh.

I hear someone say, *I want some of that FEMA's money.*

They don't know FEMA is not a person.

Maybe we can find Daddy today.

Daddy will like Atlanta. Maybe he'll even come for us.

I like the idea of staying in Atlanta while our house is repaired.

My chest feels warm. Sammie is dancing with a wide smile on her face.

What's Up?

—Sammie

Hey.   What's your name?

Where you from?

Y'all just got here from New Orleeens?

Where your parents at?   They dead?

Who you with?   You wanna hit this?   What grade you in?

You got a man?   Where all your stuff?

I heard on tv that Katrina flooded the whole city.

What's a levee?   Why you didn't go to the Dome?

We got a Dome in Atlanta.   What school you go to?

My cousin live in New Orleeens.

We ain't heard from her yet.   You cute.

You wanna go with us?

You know where you going?

Ya'll got this song on the radio in New Orleeens?

Who you listen to?

What grade you in?

You got some money?

You want some of this?

You know where you going?

Alone

—Ronnie

The forms they want me to fill out

don't make much sense.

One volunteer thinks I'm grown.

I tell her I am seventeen.

She blinks embarrassment away.

I remember when Mamma said we had her family's genes.

Daddy looked past Mamma on the couch.

He put his finger in the air.

Watch out for nasty boys trying take your purity, he warned.

Sammie scrunched up her nose.

What is that?

Mamma threw her head back and laughed real loud.

That's your innocence, baby. Don't worry about it.

You'll know when someone tries to take

what he ain't supposed to have,

and you'll know when to give it to the right man some day.

Then she looked at Daddy and winked.

That's when I figured out what love looks like.

Chapter 3

Center of Attention

—**Treasure**

At the Southside Rec Center

I watch a girl get off one of the buses from New Orleans.

She looks all around her like she is in outerspace.

Or an orphan from one of those old black and white movies

my grandmother likes to watch on Sundays.

Everbody's talking about Hurricane Katrina.

A thousand people coming to Atlanta everyday, they say.

I just came to help out 'cause I don't have anything to do today.

Nice day like this, and I don't have anything to do.

They have me stuffing bags with socks and bottled water.

I just listen to my music, try not to think about all these people

who need all these socks.

I wonder what it's like to lose everything.

To lose my nice clothes, Buckhead apartment, Tre.

I had nothing before Tre. Just like that song on the radio:

"I wasn't nothing till I met you…ooh, girl. You know that's true."

The girl is in the parking lot now. She is in the center of a circle of boys.

She's so pretty. And tall. She looks back at the building

at someone she can't leave. I know that look.

I like this bench by the courts because of the shade.

I like to watch people, too. Nobody notices me over here.

I see the girl dancing. She is bouncing to the songs

in between sips of soda. The boys want her to go with them.

She is like a little bird who is too scared to leave the nest.

Sometimes Tre sings me a song about a bird

when we get home late. He calls me his songbird.

In Line

—Ronnie

I know we have to go or end up in foster care.

I can not let that happen.

In foster care they beat children.

I remember reading about a girl who was molested in foster care.

But what can we do?

Daddy never told us much about our family.

We have aunts and uncles. I only know their first names.

How will the Red Cross find "Uncle Jackson" or "Aunt Birdie"?

My chest is hard like metal.

I two-step to the table. It's the same smiling lady

I've been avoiding. I ask about Daddy.

She will not tell me anything.

Her nail polish is chipped and dandruff sits on her shoulders.

A chorus of voices drowns her out.

I can tell she wants me to be an easy fix.

But I insist on finding Daddy. She wants me out of her line.

She sends me to the children's room after stamping my papers.

The room is filled with babies and kids.

A girl my age looks at my clothes and hair

as if I am in a disguise. I tell her about my sister.

I gotta get her, I say.

The girl doesn't want to talk to me.

You supposed to wait in here, right?

I am ready to fight her if I have to.

I figured out that I know that information

is worth fighting for.

Little Girl Grown

—Treasure

She is coming to the bench now.

Her clothes are wrinkled.

She sits next to me.

Her jeans are too small.

Her hair is a mess.

Now she is staring at my Louis Vuitton purse

but she doesn't know if it is real.

She asks me why I am at the center.

I don't want her to know that I used to live

in this neighborhood. My old stomping ground.

She doesn't need to know that I work out at the gym

if Tre says I need to lose a few pounds.

The white people in our building

stare at me too much when I go to the workout room.

So I stay away.

I flex my biceps for her. She smiles like a little girl.

Then she traces the strap of my purse with one finger.

She asks if I am a dancer.

What you mean by exotic? Like a bird?

Then I see how old she is. Just like that.

She squints like the sun

is in her eyes, but there is only shade.

She asks me how old I am.

I'm eighteen. Like you, right?

She laughs a little and rubs her eyes.

Then she looks at the building.

I feel sorry for her.

She is like a little girl left on the steps at school.

Tre's voice is swimming in my head now:

You'll see, girl. People have short memories.

You help somebody one day

and they'll stab you in the back the next.

I tell her she can come home with me.

My place will impress her.

You can bring me back? she says, walking backkward

toward the center. I keep thinking she

will trip, but she just turns around

and skips all the way to the building.

That makes me hum a favorite song:

"I'm walking on sunshine…yeah yeah yeah…"

Hot and Tired

—Sammie

I got to tell Ronnie about Treasure.

She got to meet her.

But I don't see her nowhere.

She say I can go with her. I know Ronnie

wanna go too. She don't want to stay here

with all these people begging for food and money.

We can go with Treasure. She can help us.

Where is she? She always somewhere reading.

It's hot and I'm tired. I'm not waiting no more.

Ready?

— Treasure

Now I have to clear it with Tre.

He will like her. He will like this little bird.

I'm so glad he answered the phone.

I can tell he is listening this time.

Sometimes when I call, if he is watching tv

he will not say much. This time is different.

Hey, hey! Treasure? How old is she?

Eighteen, I say.

"I couldn't imagine a love more true…baby, baby, now that I have you."

New Start

—Wilson

The people in charge of the database said the girls were not in Texas or Virginia. That's all they could tell me. That's all. Why wouldn't the girls be in the system? They got in the helicopter, so why wouldn't they be at one of the shelters? The lady looked me in the eye. *You have to report them as missing with some agency if I want to find them.* If? Who wouldn't want to find their own children? I got mad as hell. I had to believe they would stay together. Ronnie would make sure of that.

I'm with my old friend Freddie in Chicago. He bought me a plane ticket right after we spoke. Good old Freddie. *Come to Chicago, man. You know I got you! But no booze. Can't have the wifey getting mad, man.* Freddie's sober now. His wife don't take no stuff. *Cool, man. Thanks.* No booze, just a straight life. Just go to work and back home. I can do that. For Velma, for the girls.

I watch the tv news everyday. Folks around the country want to help the victims. Everything is gone. The house, all my stuff. Maybe I can do this. Get it together and find my girls, too.

Gone

—Ronnie

Outside the center, the Georgia air is still.

I see people walking, standing, waiting

but I can tell their voices are muted

by their frantic thoughts.

I don't see Sammie.

Maybe she thought

she could go to someone's house and

come back before I would miss her.

Daddy is always sending me out to find her.

I sit down on a bench and wait.

People stare at the evacuees. At me.

I am not who I used to be. Even these clothes feel funny.

I decide not to cry as the fear in my chest

turns to a large wave. *Where are you, Sammie?*

I was in charge of Sammie

and now she is gone. Daddy's gone.

And now the sun is leaving, too.

My body is falling asleep, part by part.

My legs and arms are like liquid.

Now I can not stop the sleep. Just like the wave.

Chapter 4

Living Large

—Treasure

In the lobby of my building, the girl's eyes

are so big. I think she is going to scream.

She grabs my arm in the elevator.

You live here? For real? she asks.

Yeah. I mean, I have roommates, but yeah.

Girl, you got that kind of money? Her eyes are Christmas-day big.

When I met Melody, that's how I looked at her.

Her red high heels and long leather coat

made me stare at her. We were in the grocery store.

Her make-up was perfect. When we talked, she asked me what

I wanted out of life. Nobody ever cared about my life.

I told her about my family—

how I didn't want to be somebody's baby mamma

still living at home. She took me to meet Tre.

And now I'm going to help this girl.

I feel like singing something happy.

So I clap my hands to hear my bracelets jingle.

New Blood
—**Tre**

What's up? Who's this?

Seeing baby girl walk through the door

makes me think of the red dress Treasure just bought.

Yeah, eye candy, for sure. Tall and stacked. The clients will like her.

I tell the girls not to crowd her. Give her some space.

Take her to get something to eat, let her watch tv.

Melody takes her to the bedroom to show her some clothes.

Bet she don't know any of those labels.

This is going to be interesting.

What happened to your family? They still in New Orleans? I ask.

Can't tell if she's lying. But I don't care.

Long as she wanna make some money, it's fine.

Girl, you are too pretty to be up in some shelter.

Why don't you stay here with us?

We'll help you get back on your feet .

Yeah, you with family now.

Hershey Bar

—Sammie

That Tre guy is so cute. Look like them old school R&B singers.

All dark skinded and tall like a big old Hershey bar.

I get a little squirmy in my stomach looking at him.

Nothing like my last boyfriend, DeVontae.

Even has a beard. DeVontae ain't got no beard.

Hershey Bar is rich. He gave me $100 like change.

Ronnie would have left by now.

No, she wouldn't even be here.

But that's why she don't have no boyfriend.

I always have boys calling me back home.

Melody and Treasure is so nice and pretty.

Treasure look just like Tyra Banks, like a supermodel.

I knew she was a model before

she even told me. She even let me try on her clothes.

I hope Ronnie is still at the center.

I'll go back tonight. Bring her a new outfit

and the money from Hershey Bar.

Treasure say I look lovely in her red dress.

Fatigue

—Ronnie

The shelter people are trying

to round up the evacuees who are left.

Another night in another shelter.

Somehow I have managed to stay un-registered.

I stay far from the line, my feet tap to some made-up rhythm.

People are starting to leave. Boxes and paper and folders

are pushed and stacked. I try to steady my breathing

but it is like being under water a few seconds too long.

I know that I cannot go anywhere without Sammie.

I can feel sleep ascend again.

I close my eyes and think about what

Mamma would say. Then I get mad for a second.

Why would Mamma visit Sammie's dreams and not mine?

Chapter 5

Broken Bird

—Hasina

The sister looks scared. She could use a friend.

I ask her to tell me her name. She hesitates.

I don't blame her. I am a stranger. But the Lord has

placed her in my path. Just look at that plastic bag.

The buses pass and she never looks up.

Bless this child, Lord.

I offer her a ride, but she has no place to go.

The storm has blown her away from home.

Oh, He works in such mysterious ways.

This broken bird has been sent to me for healing.

A Stranger in Need

—Ronnie

I watch the sun make its exit.

This neighborhood changes too.

Kids and adults come out of nowhere.

Cars cruise up and down the street.

There is a parade of thumping, shiny cars.

Boys are hanging in the parking lot across the street

where the line for chicken and fish sandwiches grows.

Hunger nudges my stomach to a groan.

Girls in shorts walk slowly past me.

Some of them have little children with them.

It is a lot like home, but not unfamiliar.

Two women with long skirts are passing out food.

They are looking for the homeless

who come to the center when it closes.

One of them looks at me, then holds up the sandwich

like a peace offering. I am so hungry.

But I don't know if hunger trumps trust.

The food in the center is gone.

I have three dollars.

Sweet Dreams

—**Sammie**

Dinner was so good! I ain't had no lobster

since we went to dinner with one of Daddy's friends last year.

Tonight Treasure paid for my food. She drank wine

the way Mamma use to—with her pinky finger up.

I need to take a nap. The $100 is in my back pocket...

I put my hand on it just to make sure...

Treasure and Melody are the big sisters I always wanted...

Ronnie is still my sister...But they are so different. And pretty...

I'm so sleepy...I can't wait to tell Ronnie. And show her the penthouse...

And let her meet Tre... and...

Home for Now

—Ronnie

I don't see how I can say no. She has a bible in her hand.

Mamma always said that you should put your trust in the Lord.

Right now, Hasina is the closest thing to that.

She is offering me a ride.

I can't stop crying. She just smiles. For a second

under that street light, she looks like Mamma.

She is tall, just like Mamma

and there is kindness in her smile--

that look that makes you feel warm inside

like when your mother holds you during a bad storm

or when a good book makes you look up from the pages

 just to think about what you just read.

Mamma has sent her to rescue me.

Angels can do things like that.

Hasina has taken me to a place she calls "The Village."

In the car I think I fell asleep for a while.

Outside the window, the neighborhood sleeps.

We pass block after block.

The trip seems long. Hasina says we are going to the West End.

It doesn't matter, but I nod anyway.

I can smell the lavender on her skin.

She lets me lean against her shoulder.

Atlanta streets are wide and long.

The lights flicker as we move through the city.

When we are in front of a group of small buildings

I ask Hasina where we are.

Home.

Little Sister

—Treasure

That girl was so impressed with the restaurant.

We didn't spend a whole lot

just enough. Tre wants us to talk to her

about staying, about modeling.

I don't think she will say no.

She says she has to talk to somebody.

I tell her to make up her own mind.

You're grown, right? So you have to take care of yourself.

I sing her a line from one of my favorite songs:

"You are everything, and everything is you..."

Easy Money

—Tre

I get back to the apartment, and those girls

are watching tv. I can tell this new girl is trouble.

I don't know why, but I can tell. Yep, I just know.

But I can see some big money coming.   Big money.

I ask her if she wants to work for me.

She doesn't understand what a model is.

You go to party, like an escort, I say.

With who?

Clients. Who else? Look, here's how it works.

I set up the dates, and you go with them.

You get to go to fancy restaurants, celebrity parties, things like that.

The girl looks clueless. Then Treasure tries to explain.

Girl, last week, I went to a dinner party with a famous actor.

Who? Who? Baby girl is pulling on Treasure's arm.

Let's just say, he's definitely on the A-list, Treasure laughs.

Everything is new to her. I like that.

She reminds me of Tracey, my little sister.

It's done, I say. I'm walking out the door. Then I turn around.

And let's work on that name.

New Life

—Sammie

Last night was crazy fun.

This morning I think about asking Tre

to take me to the center.

I can't let them know about Ronnie.

I want this to be mine.

Not ours. I want my own job.

If they see her, they will want her, too.

And the way she yelled at me. Shoot.

She made me so mad. She ain't my mamma.

Mamma never yelled at me.

And anyway, Ronnie always taking care of me.

So it's time for me to take care of me.

Hershey Bar say he can buy anything I need.

Keep moving. Keep moving.

He even got my first job planned.

Today we suppose to spend the whole day

at a beauty shop. Treasure and Melody

are teaching me how to eat at fancy

restaurants, how to walk like a model.

Crazy fun. Hershey Bar will be happy

and Daddy will faint when he sees

me all grown up. He's going to want to

take my picture, without Ronnie.

Not Home

—Ronnie

I don't remember going to bed last night.

Just waking up to the sounds

of pots and pans and the smell of food.

I heard birds chirping outside my window.

But my chest was calm.

I am in a strange room in a strange bed

like Goldilocks in Atlanta.

I hear women down the hall.

Please let Hasina be with them, I pray secretly.

I can hear a door open and close. Then more chatter.

They are in a good mood. Somebody is humming.

One woman wants to wake me up.

I can smell something sweet.

I think I hear Hasina say, *Let the child sleep.*

So Lovely

—Tre

Got started early today.

Don't want Lovely running out on me. Naw, can't have that.

Already invested money in her.

Plus, I like seeing that look on her face.

At breakfast, I tell her we have to do something

about her name. Treasure was the one who

came up with "Lovely."

She's so lovely, she said. *She's my little sister now.*

Lovely likes being Treasure's new pet.

Says she never liked her name anyway.

I know something about that.

I ask why her parents named her Sammie.

She looks down like a little kid

caught doing something wrong—

just like Tracey.

I don't have time for all this debate. Naw.

You're Lovely now. Welcome to the family.

The Big Picture

—Wilson

Those people at the Red Cross must be losing their minds if they think I believe that! No record of the girls? I saw them take my girls up in a helicopter. Hell, I wasn't that damned drunk! Then they hang up. Just like that. I got to go down there. Damned website don't have no information. How can they lose two little girls?

But I'm grateful. The local paper wants me to do some part-time work. When the guy said I could work, I thought I had hit the jackpot. *This is going to get me back to my girls*, I thought. A steady gig, no drinking. Now I just gotta get a place for us. The editor liked my shots from the shelter. Said he wanted to do something with it. *Not too many of those people made it to Chicago*, he said. *But I want to show the devastation, the desperation.* He smiled. Thoughts flooded my mind. *Why is he smiling? Nothing funny about desperate folks. Nothing funny about waiting for state troopers to rescue you from the roof of a church while your children cry for their dead mamma 'cause they know you can't do nothing for them.* Nothing at all.

Chapter 6

—Lovely

It's so weird when people call me Lovely.

Three weeks now and it's still weird.

I keep forgetting to answer.

What would Ronnie think? Where is she?

My mind is a jigsaw puzzle. I think about my room

back home with all my stuff. Ms. Jackie's rose garden.

Treasure's silly smile. Mamma's soft hands. How hot

it was on that roof. How mean I was to Ronnie on the bus.

But none of it will fit.

I like knowing I can find Ronnie anytime I want to.

Plus, Tre said he called those FEMA people and they want us to wait

a while before we go down there. I don't know where that is,

but Tre say he know everything.

Those volunteer people must have Ronnie on the website.

They probably sent everybody on them buses to a shelter, except me.

And I like that. Nobody know who I am or where I am.

It's like I'm a spy.

Treasure and Melody and Tre don't even know my last name.

They just want me to be a part of their family.

I wish them stupid girls from school could see me.

I got clothes they ain't even heard of.

Versachee and Armanee and Prayda.

If them girls at school knew how I was living now

they would want me to sit with them in the cafeteria.

I wonder if any of them is here in Atlanta.

Mamma would like Treasure.

She is like my big sister. And Tre is like my big brother.

Me and Ronnie use to pray for a big brother when we was little.

Angels

—Ronnie

The ladies from the kitchen wear white. All white.

White shirts, white skirts,

white scarves on their heads, white shoes.

My first day with them reminded me of being in a hospital.

I don't know their language about God, though.

My jeans and red t-shirt made me feel guilty

but for what? I am grateful when they feed me

 and ask about my church and parents.

Their eyes sparkle whenever I talk about New Orleans.

Everyday I ask them to take me to the center and check with the Red Cross.

Sometimes they say yes, but then they look at Hasina.

I have left messages with everyone on your behalf.

Hasina's voice is as soft as her skin.

Nobody has called back. They say there are people in shelters

and in homes all throughout Georgia.

We'll keep looking for her.

Then we all pray.

When I can, I make calls myself. I even got online

at the library once and put started a My Space page.

Daddy might check. He might.

No Pimpin'

—Tre

Little girl, I told you already. I get hired by clients to provide a service.

That service involves pretty girls. Making sure that I have pretty girls

at the parties and in the studios and video shoots.

She doesn't understand, keeps looking down, shaking

one leg crossed over the other. Every now and then she looks up at

me with mean eyes, like she's mad.

Still trying to be grown.

Crazy girl keeps calling me a pimp.

I mean, yeah, I come from a family of pimps and strippers.

Hell, some of the women in my own family are strung out

on drugs and alcohol.

Most of my little cousins get passed from one relative to another.

Not me, though. Naw. I left my mother's house as soon as I could.

She made me promise that I would graduate from

high school, and I did.

 After that, I had two choices:

become a pimp like my uncle

or work for a music studio as a janitor. This guy I knew

hooked me up with a job.

My uncle just knew I would

want the money from the hustle.

But I hate being in the street. Too unpredictable.

So I mopped and scrubbed and cleaned after

guys who thought they would be millionaires from one song.

Now those fools are hoping and rapping, and I'm straight.

Nothing illegal about providing eye candy.

Movin' On Up

—Gigi

My, my, my. That's all I can say when I come to this apartment.

All up in the white folks land of plenty. That Tre is a trip and a half.

He got these girls up in a highrise looking good. I mean good!

Every time I come, I just shake my head.

Some brothers talk the talk, but he means what he says.

Gonna make some real money without working for somebody else.

And look at him. He got his own accountant, lawyer, and a personal assistant.

The boy done good. He done real good for himself.

Booster

—Sammie

Hershey Bar is nice. But I told him I wasn't having sex with nobody.

Treasure say she has fun at the parties.

Girl, it ain't all that. You get dressed up and hang out

with producers and wanna-be hip-hop stars.

She say sometimes you have to "work the door."

That mean you have to play hostess.

I ask her how much I can make doing this.

She say you have to be smart with your money.

I bet you have a lot of money by now, huh?

She don't know anything about saving, just spending.

Most of the clothes are bought from a booster anyway.

You mean somebody stole all that stuff?

Girl, ain't nobody asking. You just pick out what you want.

From where?

From Gigi. She comes by every month with bags of stuff. You'll see.

His Will

—Hasina

The little sister is beautiful.

Like my Khadijah.

The Lord has truly heard my prayers.

One year to the day He took my Khadijah,

He brought me Veronique.

What more can He do?

When I tell her that I will help her find her family

it is not a lie. Family can be anyone who loves you.

And love is what I have to give.

Community

—Ronnie

Hasina wants me to stay for a few more weeks.

I worry about my family

but this family has taken me in.

I even dreamt of Mamma last night.

She had on a purple hat and those

purple and gray socks we bought her

one Christmas. She smelled like lavendar.

Maybe this is what she wants.

Hasina finally took me to the Red Cross office

but it is packed each time we visit.

At the rec center, they said the Red Cross is not coming back.

The church people don't watch tv, so I don't know

where other people from home are living.

Some nights I stay up and cry,

but then I fall asleep thinking of Mamma.

The clothes they gave me come from the church's warehouse.

They own a bank, apartments, a grocery store, everything.

We're just a little community within a community.

The Lord has given us several blocks

to call our own, so we do the best we can with it.

Where do all of the kids go to school? I ask.

At the church's school, and we have a day care center for the babies.

What about jobs? Does anybody work?

Yes, if you're 16 or older you will be given a job.

We have to use the talents God has given us.

This doesn't sound anything like my church.

Our pastor helps people when he can.

Hasina's hand covers mine

as we sip tea and look out the kitchen window.

I feel light when she's with me.

In my chest I feel an easy ripple in a quiet lake.

Firsts

—**Tre**

Victory. That's what I felt when I scored my first client.

I had spent a lot of time going to all the clubs,

meeting the promoters, talking up the bartenders, stuff like that.

It worked. Yeah. The girls were a hit.

At first it was mainly listening parties or print ads.

You know, every rapper likes to be photographed with sexy ladies.

My girl Melody was just what they liked.

She didn't mind wearing close to nothing either.

Got a body like a super model but the attitude of a 'hood rat.

But she didn't have experience with modeling.

One night a guy came up to her in Primal.

Asked her about being a hostess

at a private party. Yep, I knew we were about to make

some good contacts and some real money then.

All she had to do was greet people at the door

and keep 'em drinking. Anybody could do that. But see,

Mel didn't want folks thinking she was a prostitute.

I told her this dude was legit. After that, he hired her

and all my girls for his events.

I had to hire more girls.

So I found some cuties from my old neighborhood.

But you gotta be careful with who you hire.

They got to represent.

After a while, I just decided to work with a couple of girls.

By the time Treasure came on board,

I had the girls working every week, even for corporate clients.

Downtown business boys love to take a hot girl to a dinner party.

Straight up!

The girls look good and have a nice time.

Then they sleep and shop during the day.

Not a bad life, you know?

My uncle wouldn't know about that. Treating ladies right.

Listen! Listen!

—Wilson

The woman at the FEMA office is nice enough to listen to me. Nobody else is willing. No word from my girls. I put their names in the missing children database.

How can I explain my actions? I left my beautiful daughters to fend for themselves in the middle of a crisis. Too drunk to get up from that rooftop. I just didn't care. I've been telling my story at the AA meetings once a week. Every week I tell a little more about what happened to our family. How my wife died and how I lost my mind for years after that. How the girls raised themselves, thanks to Ronnie. How my business went under and we lived off food stamps and the life insurance from the accident. How I blamed God 'cause my wife didn't have to die. How life is sometimes a spiral you can't seem to stop. I told these strangers the story of my life. Same thing I told the FEMA lady. And they listened. That's all that mattered.

Chapter 7

Straight and Clean

—Wilson

The card is full. It's been two months since we floated out of New Orleans. Freddie helped me get hired with a landscaper. Can't live off taking pictures. Now I can pay Freddie for the room. Then save enough money to get to the girls. Maybe that FEMA money will come soon. I even started going to meetings for my drinking. And church. Met some nice people in Freddie's church. Most nights I count down the weeks, check the database for the girls, and read. I keep a journal, too. I write letters to Velma. Somehow I know she's watching the girls. I asked her to forgive me. What was I thinking, letting them go like that? I have to find them. I have to let them know how I've been living. Straight and clean. Straight and clean.

Prayers

—Ronnie

They do everything the same way: pray, sing, hold hands, testify.

But with a smile. Most of the people in my

church never smile. Maybe being on the Lord's side is so

serious that you can't be happy, at least not in church.

And they don't separate the kids from the adults.

Sitting next to me today is a lady and her three kids.

Her husband plays the piano like a man

I once saw through a hotel bar window.

He's playing with his eyes closed,

smiling at something only he can see.

His wife is smiling at me and the children.

Sometimes, he opens his eyes and smiles at them.

She reaches over to share her bible with me.

Her wedding band is plain and dull.

Her kids are little. And quiet. Almost too quiet.

Sammie and I used to get in trouble for playing in church.

But these kids are sitting patiently for almost two hours.

I can't wait to tell Sammie, especially about

the cute boy who smiles at me from the choir.

Lonely

—Sammie

Being a twin mean you can feel what your twin feel.

It mean you not alone even when your twin ain't around.

I don't want to lose Ronnie, but I don't know how to find her.

Plus, things is going too good. That may sound stupid, but it's true.

Katrina came when things was going good.

And things was good with our family when Mamma died.

So you never know.

Trey is watching some special about Katrina people in Atlanta,

how they surviving on food stamps and waiting

for their FEMA money.   He's nodding his head like somebody talking to him.

Those people on tv is living in shelters.

I feel like crying sometimes when I about leaving Ronnie.

I pretend she in my room sometime.

I talk to her like she sitting right at the edge of my bed.

If the Red Cross don't know where she is,

will I see her again? That make me feel lonely.

First daddy, now Ronnie.

Tre said not to worry about finding Daddy 'cause

he talked to them FEMA everyday.

He said he told them I was here.

He said they want me to wait some more.

Wait….Wait

—Ronnie

Hasina has been gone for two days. At first, I think she has gone

to look for Daddy and Sammie. She promised she would.

The other women tell me she has gone to Macon, Georgia,

where her mother lives. For a second, I feel afraid.

What if she has left me?

I have learned that everyone's truth is not always my truth.

I am not always sure of what to believe here.

Here in Atlanta, the ground is not solid

and I fear I will be swallowed up one day.

The cute boy from the choir wants to help me find Sammie.

Norman. Norman is a nice name. A normal name. Normal Norman.

He is my age and has been raised in the church. He is tall, like a basketball player.

But he doesn't play sports. He likes to draw.

He has dreadlocs and dark skin. His eyes are light brown.

I could look at him all day.

At the car, when he opens my doorm, warmth floods my chest.

Little Sister

—Treasure

Lovely is our little sister now.

She belong to me and Melody and Tre.

We are a family.

She ain't going nowhere.

At least, I hope not.

She has us, so why would she go back?

She keeps talking about her father.

Probably homesick. That's ok, 'cause we are her family now.

She has to believe that.

"We are family…nah, nah, nah, nah, nah, naaaahhh…"

A New Friend

—Ronnie

Every weekend, Norman takes me to the rec center to look for Sammie.

Today we are standing at the front desk. We have been here for five minutes.

but no one seems to be working. Finally a man comes around the corner.

He is wearing a t-shirt with the name of the center on it.

His glasses sit at the tip of his nose. His belly rests on top of his belt buckle.

He tells us he has not seen anyone who looks like Sammie.

Did you come in from Louisiana?

I am too afraid to tell him the truth.

No, I just had some relatives who were here and I need to find them.

I can't look at Norman. I know he does not approve of lying.

The man says we should go to the police.

My chest freezes. Too much paperwork could mean foster care.

Norman shakes his head. He seems to understand.

On the drive to the Village, he tells me about his family.

His profile reminds me of Daddy's. His hands grip the wheel

as he talks with pride about his mother.

She left his father when Norman was three.

That's when they joined the church.

So you came here like I did?

I like Norman in this moment. He is gentle with his words.

I imagine he is like Daddy used to be when he first met Mamma.

Not My Mother

—Gigi

In the mirror someone else stares back at me.

It is my mother.

People always tell me I look just like her.

I still don't want to believe it.

I put my jacket on, grab my garment bags

and head out for the day. Time for the hustle.

Thoughts of my mother are now deep frowns.

I can't seem to stop frowning.

My mamma is not half the mother I am, I say to myself.

My daughter, Chalyse, loves me and she knows I love her.

We don't need nobody to tell us how to live or love.

When I pass my old apartment building

I stop frowning so much. There were some good times here.

Even after my father passed. I think about the family

that lives in our old unit. Is there a girl in my bedroom?

Is she staring at the water mark in the ceiling the way I did?

I load the bags into my car. The sounds of kids on their way to school,

vendors selling fruit and shea butter and t-shirts

and the slow, loud buses pass by.

My mother warned me to stay away from "the streets."

That's where the bad girls end up. In "the streets."

But the streets is where I have learned

the hard way that love don't care about your past.

Love is the only free thing in this world

if you are willing to fight for it.

Whirlwind

—Sammie

Treasure don't want me to find Ronnie. I can tell.

But I have to let her know I'm ok.

I tried the Red Cross number but calls go to voice mail.

How can you tell somebody that your family is missing?

Sometimes when we don't have to work, I take long baths

and think about home. Mamma don't come to my dreams now.

Maybe she too busy with Ronnie.

Tre too busy trying to get us ready for New York.

He say this is going to be a money making trip

like no other. Something about celebrities.

I hope we get to eat lobster.

Trey said he needed to find Gigi.

She only come by once a month.

Her bags is always stuffed with purses bags and shoes

from those high price stores at the mall.

She make me laugh when I tell her about home.

She say she want to taste some gumbo and them little doughnuts.

I thought that was funny.

Beignets? Girl, you need to eat some king cake!

She the only person that tells me to keep looking for Daddy.

Out of Place

--Gigi

Those girls are too much for me!

Everyday they sit around the apartment all made up

like they have somewhere to go.

Then they hit the clubs.

I know they aren't breaking any laws, but they need to be in school.

That's what I tell Tre. He doesn't want to hear it.

I'm not forcing them to stay. That's all he can say.

That new one is sweet though.

Lovely.

I asked Tre about her family.

I know she's not from our neighborhood.

And she always looks sad.

He looked like he was about to say something nasty.

So I started packing up my stuff.

Sometimes he gets that look in his eyes

just like his crazy uncle. I know that look.

Men who have that look don't look at you.

Just through you.

But Tre knows right from wrong.

He knows mercy is a step from grace.

Business First

—Tre

Lovely keeps asking me about finding her father.

I have to figure this out. We have to go

to New York for the big fight this week.

I need at least ten girls for that trip.

I already have a request for Lovely.

This is business. Family can wait.

I just keep telling her that those FEMA folks say

she should wait. And that's what she does.

Answered Prayers

—Hasina

Norman and Veronique remind me of my youth

Their love is growing stronger

along with her faith.

Veronique has a kind heart.

And she's so smart.

She even has a job at the school.

The teachers love her, the children too.

Now when I say my prayers for Khadijah,

I add a prayer for Veronique.

What good is a mother's love without a child to give it to?

Reflection

—Gigi

Every morning I look in the mirror

to convince myself of what must be true:

I am a good mother because my daughter gets good grades.

Because I make sure her friends come from good families.

Because I am on the PTA. Because I make time for her.

And every morning I think of my mother.

I think of how much she is missing. How she kicked me out

of the house when I told her I was pregnant. How she stopped

being my mother when I stopped sharing her faith.

My mother would love her granddaughter

but she has never seen or touched her. She does not know

how Charlyse's laughter makes your heart flutter. Or how

her eyes twitch when she's sleeping. She does not know

what a grandmother should know about herself: that who we

wish we were becomes the promise in our children.

These thoughts swirl about me whenever I see her

in the West End. I used to look for her. Now I pretend

to not look. I dash in and out, trying to avoid the people

from my youth. But today I wasn't so lucky.

And here I am, staring at her right now

watching her through the bakery window across the street.

She stands straight as a tree, bible in hand.

Chalyse is trying to pull me across the street.

But I can't move.

My mother's profile looks

like a statue in a museum.

Like a kid, I want to touch the marble smoothness.

Flashback

—Wilson

Hello. My name is Wilson. And I'm an alcoholic.

Sometimes I dream of the girls. That's when all the memories I tried to drink away start to flood my mind like the waters that separated us. I can see them. Looking like their mother. I can hear the helicopter's loud whir, even feel the hot concrete and crunchy gravel beneath me as I sat on that rooftop. The whisky was sour and sweet in my mouth. I just wanted to stay there or be taken away with the water. Just taken away. I wanted my Velma. My legs felt like stones too heavy to move. I squeezed that damned bottle, but what I wanted was to hold my girls. They went up in that helicopter so fast. Now I can see the fear in their eyes. That day, I could only see their faces. But now I can see their eyes. Just fear.

Conversion

—Ronnie

When the church sings, I feel warm.

My hands tingle and a light glows from my chest.

Maybe everyone can see it, I don't know.

But I feel it. Today was even more special.

The pastor came to me, right at the end of service.

He touched my forehead and closed his eyes.

And there it was! A light so strong I had to close my eyes, too.

It showered me with love.   I felt weak and then swept up

by someone, the way Daddy used to gather me from the couch

when I'd fall asleep watching tv. I felt safe.

When I opened my eyes, I was in the church office.

Hasina stood over me with a glass of water.

You're ok, child, she said.

Lavendar filled the room. I could feel her warm hand on mine.

Headed for Home

—Wilson

When the ancestors came to me in a dream, they had different faces. Some I knew, but there was only one voice. They prayed for me and the girls. A light mist covered me, soft and moist.   I saw Velma, too. She smiled like nothing was wrong. *Oh, Velma,* I cried. *Where you been? Come back to us, baby.* When I woke up, I had Summer Hill on my mind. Then a check was in the mail. FEMA sent me a check. Now I'm going home. Yes! I'm going home!

Chapter 8

Offer

— Hasina

Veronique is ready to join. The Lord told me so.

Last night, He told me to speak to her.

So I am here, at the edge of her bed.

Books are scattered about her.

I recall some titles from my youth.

Just like my Khadijah, I thought.

Always reading and studying.

We want you to know that you are welcome here, I say.

I know, Ms. Hasina, she answers quietly. She looks down at the bed.

The Church can offer you so much, Veronique. Not just spiritual comfort and guidance.

But what about my family? She is rubbing her chest slowly.

Yes, they called. The other week. I couldn't tell you. The pain of losing your family--
She is crying harder. I place her hand in mine.

The Red Cross confirmed that your father didn't make it. I believe he died in his sleep.

And the police have found someone in the city morgue who matches your sister's description.

I can feel the Lord's spirit in the room. It is strong like a mighty storm gathering behind me.

If this is not His will, surely I will not live to see tomorrow.

Veronique is paralyzed with grief before me.

I lift her face to meet her eyes.

We have so much to offer you, Veronique. Please, let us help you.

Big Love

—Ronnie

Gone. Daddy and Sammie. Just gone. Mamma. Daddy. Sammie.

I thank God for Hasina and her big heart.

It is big enough to swallow me whole.

She just may be a real angel sent from Mamma.

Some people call themselves angels, but they are not so divine.

I know she has a daughter. I've seen pictures of her.

Norman said something about her once.

She left the church, he said. That was it.

When I asked why, he was quiet.

I know that kind of quiet-- secret kind of quiet.

You don't ask questions about it.

Norman turned to me. *Some people break your heart*

but they do it to save their own.

It's been just a few months and I already have

a job and my own room.

I always hated sharing with Sammie.

A room of my own for all of my books.

For some peace.

The church is helping me finish school.

They will help me go to college if I join.

They have members in the admissions office

at the community college.

God has willed it, they say.

There are days when staying here makes me very happy.

Daddy and Sammie would be happy for me, right?

On good days, I dream of finding Daddy and Sammie

and bringing them here.

There's nothing to worry about when you're here.

Whenever Norman takes me for walks,

even the thugs step aside.

It is not fear, just respect.

The church keeps the park clean

and feed the homeless.

They keep to themselves but give so much

to others. Mamma would like that.

I place my hand on my chest.

No currents or waves.

Just a trickle of happiness.

Mirage

—Gigi

Back in the West End. Again.

Seems like I'm always somewhere I don't want to be.

Today, I had to get burgers at Al's

for Chalyse. That's our thing.

She studies and I make, or get, dinner.

Today, I am not up to cooking.

That's how I am different from my mother.

She bakes perfect cakes and pies,

my microwave popcorn burns.

Sometimes I stand in front of the stove

and imagine I am her, humming some song

from church.

Today the cool air forces its way

between people on the street. We are all in its way.

The light changes. Nobody notices me, or they pretend

to not notice me. Either way, I'm fine.

Their sideways glances don't bother me.

I walk across the street to my car

but now I am staring at Lovely.

Wait a minute!

Is it Lovely? Looks like her. Same pretty face.

I have to blink to make sure. She is sitting in the coffee shop.

What's she doing over here?

She looks me dead in the eye.

Not even a smile.

Just like I'm a stranger.

I almost yell, *Girl, what you doing here?*

Then I think about Tre.

His girls can't be caught in the old neighborhood.

Look at her clothes. Has she joined the church?

The Arc of the Redeemer.

I think she has. Look at those plain clothes.

She's sitting up straight as a pin.

Her head is wrapped tight, "keeping the devil out."

Is that Norman with her?

I remember babysitting him.

Now he's a man. Still got those dreadlocs.

I have to get over to the apartment. Something's not right.

Family Matters

—Treasure

Last night Lovely said she wanted to find her sister real bad.

That's why she looks sad all the time. She never said nothing about a sister.

I try to cheer her up.

But none of my songs cheer her up anymore.

 She works the parties and has a good time.

But at home, it's a different story.

What about your parents? I ask.

My daddy got separated from us when we got on that helicopter.

Damn. That's messed up. You call that number for the Red Cross?

Yeah, but they don't know where he is. Or Ronnie. What if I don't find them?

I don't know what to say. I try to get her excited about New York.

I tell her about the clothes, the lights, the fun. But nothing works.

I can go home any day.

But she only has us. Just us.

"Just the two of us… We can make it if we try… Just the two of us… You and I"

Whenever I fought with my cousins

my grandmother used to yell at us, *Family matters! Family matters!*

We never knew what she meant by that.

Big Dreams

—Tre

Gigi wants to come by tonight.

She always has some scam going on.

I don't have time for street games.

I've seen that kind of stuff my whole life.

I am not about to go back to small-time hustling.

I have dreams bigger than my family can ever comprehend. Yeah.

And I don't have to be a pimp or a dealer to live them.

Gigi doesn't know anything about making real money.

About building an empire. She can keep her boosting.

I am about the business. And Lovely is good business.

Just gotta get baby girl to New York, make that money

and that's all there is to it.

Love Lost

—Hasina

Veronique, I don't like to talk about her.

She has asked about my daughter, but today I can't deny her.

I always thought love was His greatest gift to us.

It doesn't cost a thing and we are all worthy of it.

But some of us just can't handle it. We use it. Throw it away.

We refuse it when we need it most. We even try to

bury it. I watched Khadijah follow it into the streets--

right out of my heart.

Tonight my Lord has granted me my greatest wish.

Veronique, my new daughter, will join us.

A second chance. A new beginning. A prayer answered.

Leaving

—Gigi

Tonight Buckhead is dark. Very dark. Not like the West End.

Seeing Lovely made my head spin. Now I'm making my way

to Tre's. I gotta know why Lovely was in the West End.

She has the right to go where she wants.

But how could she be in the church and work for him?

Plus, what if Tre finds out?

Secrets like that only end badly.

I know a little something about that.

Inside the apartment, everything's quiet.

I think of talking to Lovely first

but Trey insists that I tell him what's going on.

You don't usually come so late. What's up, Gigi?

He is heating up some leftovers for Lovely.

It's funny to see him in the kitchen.

His dress shirt and polished loafers shine under the kitchen lights.

I tell him that I have Prada and Gucci in the car.

Tre is all smiles now.

For a second we are back in the old 'hood.

He is that little kid at Al's sipping on a soda.

And I'm dipping out of bible study.

I like this moment between us.

I'm cracking him up with stories

about our old friends. *Remember Bobo? He live in the country now!*

And those Hudson kids? All of them in prison. Even their grandfather!

That's not what you came here for, is it? Tre is not laughing now.

I can't hide my nervousness. It's Trey, right? My old friend.

But the man before me is all about business. A sharp flash of fear

courses through me. Then Lovely comes out of the bedroom.

She is crying. Her hair is a mess and her clothes are wrinkled.

Lovely, what's going on here? What are you two up to?

She looks at Tre like she is scared to answer.

I wanna go home, Tre. I wanna go back home. I want my sister and my daddy!

Sister? Now I get it. The girl I saw was her sister!

I know where she is, Lovely! I can't hide my excitement.

Trey steps closer.   His cologne rushes my nose.

Where is Ronnie?   She raises her eyebrows and grabs my hands.

It feels like I won some bet and the money is about to hit my hand.

Tre just looks at me like I am losing my mind.

Baby girl, you didn't say you had a twin. So, she looks just like you?

Lovely looks like a trapped animal. Her eyes dart between us.

Tre has to sit down. He's clicking his lighter, trying to figure it all out.

But I was gonna tell you, Tre. Lovely turns to me. *Gigi, please take me to her.*

Hold up! Hershey Bar stands up.

Ain't nobody say anything about going to get her.

Let the girl see her sister, Tre. That's family, Gigi says.

I feel like I am doing what Mamma would want me to do.

Standing up to Hershey Bar.

Ain't that what Ronnie would do if she was here?

Please, Tre. I need to go to Ronnie. I need to tell her I'm sorry for leaving and I need

to ask her about Daddy—

What you need to do is work this gig tomorrow in New York, he says.

That twinkle in his eye is gone.

Baby girl, I already told you what those FEMA people said.

It seem like the room is getting smaller. He keep banging his fist against his legs

I think it might be me next. You *just gotta wait. They know you here.*

They'll call you when they find your father.

But this whole thing with your sister…I don't think it's a good idea.

Tre, just let me see her tonight. I'll come back. I'll bring her over here if you want.

I'm crying again but it don't matter.

Hershey Bar stops and points his finger in my face.

Look, you messing with my money, baby girl. You know what that mean?

He moving so close that he's in my face.

You can come and go as you like. This ain't no prison. And I ain't no pimp!

He is standing so close I can smell his breath. I keep blinking

'cause he is yelling and pointing at my head.

But understand this: you owe me a lot of money. A lot. You think these

clothes and perfume and shoes are free? Huh? You think this is all free?

He pulls on my new top. I hold my breath.

So we going on a little trip, baby girl.

You going to say goodbye to your sister, then we going to New York.

You got that? Pay off your debt, then do what the hell you want to.

I just want Daddy.

I want him to tell Hershey Bar

not to talk to me like this.

I want Ronnie to come find me.

I want Mamma to come to my dreams again.

I want to go home.

Heart, Breath

—Gigi

Looking at Sammie broke my heart.

All she wanted was her family.

I know about that kind of need.

I have Charlyse, but no one else.

When family turns their back on you

it's like being in this world with no beginning or end.

Sometimes I just sit on Charlyse's bed

while she's sleeping and stare at her.

She's my life. My heart. My breath.

Monster

—Tre

I am not a monster. I am not a pimp. I know about family.

I know that girl wants to see her family. Hell, I want to see my family

sometimes. But what good is family when they constantly disappoint?

People always telling you they love you just 'cause you family. Naw.

They lying. You can't trust nobody in this world, especially family.

She'll learn. She'll see I'm doing this for her own good.

I'm going to make Lovely a star. If she just goes to New York,

she's going to see that there are things even her family can't give her.

Chapter 9

Rescue Me

—Sammie

I have to go to New York. I ain't got no choice.

But the thought of it make me feel dizzy.

Mamma's picture is staring at me from the dresser.

Tre and Gigi is in the living room

waiting for me. What am I suppose to do?

Pack. Pack some clothes. That's right. Tre said to go pack.

He say we going to the West End

before the airport. My head is hurting.

I have to stop crying now.

He might hear me.

He might come in here.

Mama is smiling in her picture.

She don't come to my dreams anymore.

My hands is cold. Why are they so cold?

My stomach is rolling and hot.

On the radio somebody is singing about loving his girl.

What am I suppose to do?

Mama keep smiling at me.

I don't want to go to New York, Mamma.

I put her picture in my purse and turn off the light.

Tidal Wave

—Ronnie

Tonight feels like the most important night of my life.

I'm joining the church this evening. Norman and Hasina

will be by my side. I want to thank them for their support.

And I want to feel the light again. The warm, warm light.

All the angel ladies are walking ahead of me. They look like nurses.

They are dressed in white, but their bodies seem stiff.

They are smiling, but somehow their lips look like slippery rubber bands.

When I look around the church

it is not the clean, gleaming church I've known.

I can see cracks and holes for the first time.

How can that be? I have been in this building

so many times over the past few months.

Now it looks like a sad building,

like it has been used and neglected far too long.

Even Hasina looks different. Her white scarf has a snag.

The soft white fabric flows from her long black hair.

But the snag seems to be growing

as the prayer continues.

I look down at my hands.

Where have they been? Where am I?

Pictures of Daddy and Sammie flood my head.

I can't even hear Reverend James.

A tidal wave knocks me to my knees

as the church choir sings everyone into a frenzy.

The last thing I see is Hasina. There is a white light blinding me.

I feel truth pulsating through the light.

The music fades to silence. My chest floods with truth.

In the Middle

—Gigi

Sometimes you know when the right thing

to do will have bad consequences.

That doesn't mean you shouldn't do it, though.

I tell Chalyse that all the time.

If somebody picks on you, you tell the teacher.

But they may come back the next day

mad as hell 'cause you got them in trouble.

That don't matter though. You did the right thing.

I keep telling myself I am doing the right thing,

standing in front of the Church

waiting for evening devotional to end.

Tre and Lovely aren't talking. Tre keeps texting people

and Lovely is sitting in the backseat crying.

How did this happen? I only wanted to help

but this is not helping. I have made this girl's life worse.

Her bags are packed and stuffed in the back of his car.

Tre is not playing around tonight.

He barely spoke to me on the way here.

I tried to tell him the church people would ask questions.

You planning on rolling up on them? You know how they are.

Tre turned his back.

I kept telling myself that it would end well.

I even said a little prayer

before we got out the car.

Me, praying? Some habits are hard to break.

This is how I hope it will play out:

Lovely will say goodbye to her sister.

Tre will realize he can't take Lovely away from her sister.

Her sister will come to her senses

and leave these crazy church people.

They will get back to New Orleans where they belong.

The door of the church is opening.

All the church members are pouring out.

I feel like a sixteen year old girl in trouble—

like I am trying not to be seen

with the wrong somebody.

Chapter 10

Revealed

—Ronnie

In the church office there are two people looking down at me.

I am not afraid, but I am angry.

Hasina feels my anger. She looks away like a coward.

The other woman offers me water.

Reverend wants us to take you home. Service has ended early, she says.

Hasina tries to leave, but I sit up and grab her arm.

They're not gone, are they?

She looks at me and I can see a deep pool of sadness in her eyes.

This time, I am determined not to drown in them.

Come, Daughter

—Hasina

Have I foresaken you? Have I not followed my heart as you commanded?

This lost bird was brought in for shelter. I have loved her as I would my own.

My own. There is always love to give. But not all of us are ready to receive it.

Gangsters

—Tre

Lovely's sister is all covered in white, looking like a nun.

Damn! She looks just like her.

I start to say something but there are too many folks around us.

Gigi is running and crying toward some lady. That's her mother!

I remember her now.

The church people are praising God. It's getting out of my control.

Somebody is grabbing my arm.

I pull back, but there are too many of them. The dudes from the church are

all around me standing like soldiers. I know that stance. Outnumbered.

I put my hands up, back away toward the car. Color of the clothes don't matter.

A gangsta is a gangsta. Baby girl's gonna have to be left behind.

I just hope she figures it all out.

Family don't mean nothing. They always betray you.

Breaking Free

—Sammie

When Tre put his hands up

I knew everything was ok.

I can see Ronnie now.

She look so clean, so small.

I think I can hear him yelling at me

but there is a lot of noise.

These church people is singing and getting happy.

I'm not scared, though.

My sister is here and she won't let

Hershey Bar take me to New York.

Daddy always said Ronnie would take care of me.

I should've listened to her.

I feel so dirty, so bad.

Sister!

—Ronnie

Sammie looks like a model. She has on heels and fancy clothes. Her hair is longer. Too much make-up. She looks like a grown-up. We are staring at each other here while evreybody praises God and surrounds Hasina. I don't know why, but it doesn't matter. My chest is not a drowning tidal wave, but a gentle waterfall. Sammie is crying. She hugs me so tight I almost fall over. I want to grab her hand and run. But we sit on the steps of the church. Her make-up is smeared and she talks so fast I have to tell her to slow down. I hold her hand tight. Just in case.

My Bird

—Hasina

Outside the church, I see my daughter.

At first, I am not sure it is her.

This girl's hair is long and she is thin.

But it is her! My Khadijah.

People are holding me up.

I suppose I fainted inside.

Their soft voices become clearer as

I step toward Khadijah.

She is crying like she used to

when I caught her doing something wrong.

I can not hold back my tears.

Everything in His time, I think.

In this moment, the past does not matter.

I want to take back those ugly words I said.

I want to say she is welcome in my home.

I want to say I am sorry.

I want to hold my daughter--

keep her safe.

I reach for her and she comes.

Homecoming

—Gigi

I ran into my mother's arms like a two year old.

Never would have guessed this would be my response.

She chose the church over me.

Left me to the streets to raise myself.

But she would say that I left her for the streets.

Right now, though, it doesn't matter.

Now I know what she has known.

I'm sorry, Mamma. I hear myself saying over and over.

A flurry of white surrounds us.

Everyone is singing and praising God for our moment.

Even the elders smile and sing along.

Brave One

—Sammie

Ronnie keep asking me what happened.

But I just want to hug her and hold on to her tight.

We sit on the steps and I try to tell her where I been.

But the people from the church is so loud.

They are dancing and singing and praying.

Then I see that they talking about Gigi.

I think one of those women is her mother.

Ronnie say we should go.

She is pointing at some guy who is waiting by a car.

I try to wipe my face, but the tears keep coming.

I think about Mamma's picture in my purse.

Thank You

—Ronnie

Atlanta has never seemed so bright.

I look at the passing lights and they remind me of stars.

Norman is taking us to the Village to get my things.

I tell him I have to go back home.

He says he understands, but he will wait for me.

How can I ask him to wait? He has so much to do for the church.

He has plans to build a high school and a community center.

He loves his church so much. And I love him for that.

But I have to go home to look for Daddy.

And Sammie needs to get out of Atlanta.

At the bus station I give Sammie the money for the tickets.

At first, she doesn't want to leave my side. Then she walks slowly

to the counter like a little kid being punished. I know she wants to look back.

I kiss Norman for the first time.

His lips are softer than I imagined.

He holds my hands.

A wave rushes through my chest.

But this is not enough to scare me.

I am not sure if I can leave him.

Before Sammie comes back, he gives me a prayer book and a locket.

Inside is a quote from the Bible:

There is no fear in love. But perfect love drives out fear... (1 John 4:18).

Chapter 11

Back Home

—Sammie

The ride back to New Orleans was longer than the ride to Atlanta.

I don't know how, but it was.

I kept waking up 'cause the lady in front of us

was eating potato chips and candy.

The sound of the wrappers was so annoying.

Crunch! Crunch! Why don't she stop eating them things?

Then I had to smell the nasty perfume she was wearing.

Plus, Ronnie was reading, so the light was on.

She still read a lot. I didn't say anything to her, though.

But now we finally in New Orleans.

Ronnie say it's time to get off the bus.

I can't wait. I promised God that I would do better this year.

I just want to go back my real life.

Back to the park, to my friends.

When we walk out the bus station

it all look so different. I never been to the bus station before.

But something's not right. Everything look so dirty.

And the streets look like something missing.

Like a big vacuum cleaner came through and sucked everything up.

Ronnie say we have to take the city bus to the house.

When we get closer, the bus driver say

we can't go near the Ninth Ward 'cause it's gone.

Our house? Gone? *What you mean, gone?*

Ronnie don't say nothing.

I keep asking him questions.

We only been gone for a few months.

Everybody's house is gone? That's crazy.

Ronnie said we needed to eat.

We go to McDonalds down the street.

It feel like we in somebody else's dream.

I want to get back to normal, but what does that mean?

New Home, Sweet Home

—Wilson

They delivered it in no time. Soon as I said I had the down payment, they said it was ready. That's how they work it. Damned finance people. Hadn't been for that FEMA money, I'd be waiting for months, years even. I had it delivered to my property. My real property. Summer Hill. It's been months since I left my house. But now I have *my* trailer home, filled with *my* furniture, and I'm waiting for *my* family. I'll sit right here on *my* lot, to wait for the girls to come home. Velma by my side.

Lost at Home

—Ronnie

We have stayed in McDonalds too long.

Plastic seats hurt after a while. Everybody here looks anxious

as if they are waiting for something to happen at any minute.

But I think it's just the city.

It feels like the entire city is taking one big breath

but is too afraid to let it out.

The manager makes me nervous.

He checks on us three times.

He wants details.

Runaways? Hookers?

Sammie's response upsets him.

Finally, he gives up.

He mumbles something about everybody being lost in this city.

Good Life

—Wilson

Today the rain is soft. I sit inside, looking out the window. Just like the day before and the day before that. I'm just waiting. And I'll wait forever if I have to. I've fixed a pot of coffee and the smell competes with the damp air. I'm sitting on the new sofa. Feels like Velma sat down right beside me. I laugh a bit, thinking of the girls when they were little things. How Ronnie always took Sammie by the hand to play. How Sammie lost the key to the house one day when we got back from church. How those girls always ended up down the street at the Renaults' house 'cause Marielle made fresh beignets for them every other day. How we all used to pile up in our bed and watch cartoons on Saturday morning. How good life can be.

Summer Hill

—Sammie

We have to go to Summer Hill!

I just know it. I don't know how

but I know this like I know my own name.

Ronnie is so sleepy. She is laying her head down

like we used to do in kindergarten when it was nap time.

She look like she want to cry or just fall out.

She look worried, too. That ain't like her.

I tell her that we will find Daddy.

He ain't in the system, Sammie, she says.

She almost shouted at me. But I don't care.

Her voice cracks, like she want to cry.

My mind is made up.

I feel Mamma behind me, pushing.

For a second, I think about Treasure and Tre.

I wonder what they doing right now.

But I stop my thoughts 'cause we need to get some help.

If we go to the police, then we might be put in foster care.

There is still Summer Hill. Our home. Our land.

I stand up. *We have to go,* I tell her.

Everybody around us is staring.

I take Ronnie's hand. *Let's go!*

Strength

—Ronnie

The rain shows us no mercy.

We are drenched, but Sammie won't let us stop.

 She's pulling me and saying something.

That's our land! If someone try to take it, we just have to fight.

I am so tired. Thoughts of Atlanta are flooding my mind:

Had we been gone that long? Did we ever live in Atlanta?

But my stomach disagrees with every thought I have.

My chest is as hard as a shell.

I stuff my hands into my pockets, then

pull them out to trace the edges of the locket Norman gave me.

Out of the Mist

—Wilson

The rain settles to a mere mist. The warm air makes it humid. Still, I sit on the couch. Been sitting and waiting for weeks now. But today, it feels like something new is buzzing around. Kind of like anticipating something you know will show up, like a friend you haven't seen in a long time, or a phone call from a job you applied for months before. I haven't had many days like this, but I know them when I feel them. Evening falls slow and minutes pass like the even pace of my breathing. Folks are turning into shadows, walking past my new house. Some look at the trailer and shake their heads, pointing. Must be wondering who lives there. This isn't the Ninth Ward, that's for sure. My girls deserve better and I finally have it to give. I got some job prospects already. Not on no construction crew either. Yeah, this storm has passed. It's time for some living. Some real living.

Home, Now

—Ronnie

A long trailer is parked on the lot.

It looks brand new.

But it does not welcome us home.

I am sure we have made a mistake. I want to turn back

but my legs are so weak, I can barely stand.

Sammie shouts, *I told you! Somebody done started living on our land.*

Sammie's feet splash the mud puddles leading up to the door.

She runs to the cinderblocks that pass as

steps to the front door.

I feel my feet sinking, like quicksand

is grabbing hold of my ankles.

Wait! I shout. But she doesn't stop.

Her umbrella is thrown to the ground.

Then the door opens.

What's Going On?

—Sammie

I ain't afraid. I thought I would be
but I don't care who is in that trailer.
That's our land. I know what Daddy meant
when he said our family may not have much
but we got Summer Hill. Whoever is in this
trailer just have to go park somewhere else.

Revelation

—Ronnie

Daddy stands at the trailer door.

He looks older, but sober.

He smiles broadly then reaches out to hug Sammie.

Was this the same man we left on the rooftop?

I stand at the edge of the grass.

And then I swear I can see Mamma beside Daddy

like a soft haze floating mid-air.

Sammy is crying so hard, it makes me laugh.

She looks back at me.
Come on, girl! We found Daddy!

My chest is warmed to a smile

as Daddy walks toward me.

My heart thumps so loudly

it nearly drowns out his words:

Come on inside. You're home now.

My Family

—Velma

And it is as it should be. As I would have it to be.

I didn't see that car coming. And the driver didn't see me
crossing the street.

I was on my way home, looking forward to making
dinner and playing cards with

Wilson. I was too busy thinking of the girls, of
how I would take them

shopping to buy costumes for the Hal-
loween party. I didn't see

what was right in front of me.

But it doesn't matter

anymore.

Nothing matters except what

we hold dear. What we love.

I was going home that night, but

home is not a building or address.

Home is any place we can be our true selves

and be loved despite our true selves.

I miss my family. But they are home now.

We are all home now.

About the Author

Lita Hooper is a poet and YA author whose young characters are challenged but triumphant in the wake of historic events. Her work has been published in various journals, magazines, and online publications. She is the author of *Thunder in Her Voice: The Narrative of Sojourner Truth* (Willow Books). When she's not writing, taking pictures, or traveling, she teaches writing and designs online courses.